Always remember that

Aunt _____
aunt's name

loves you,

_____ ...
child's name

beary much!!!

In dedication to Elle

# Your Aunt
# Loves You
## Beary Much

Your aunt loves...
with all her heart.

More than anything,
sweet or tart.

She loves you when
you're dirty or clean.

She loves you more
than mice love cheese!

She loves spending
time together...

Even more than sunny weather!

She'll give you lots of
great big hugs.

And give you gifts
with lots of love.

She'll drive to see you,
near or far!

She'll travel out
among the stars.

You'll play lots
of games
when you're
together.

She'll take you
out for fun
things to do!

She'll grab your favorite book and read to you...

when you're with her,
she feels like she can fly.

when you leave,
it's hard to
say goodbye.

She loves you as
you drift and dream.

And she loves you more than any ice cream.

She loves you more
than bears love honey...

More than carrots
are loved by bunnies!

In all this world
there is one thing
you should know...

Your aunt loves you...
beary, beary much so!